WITHDRAWN
BY
WILLIAMSBURG REGIONAL LIBRARY

One, Two, Where's My Shoe?

Tomi Ungerer

Williamsburg Regional Library
757-259-4040   www.wrl.org

APR - - 2015

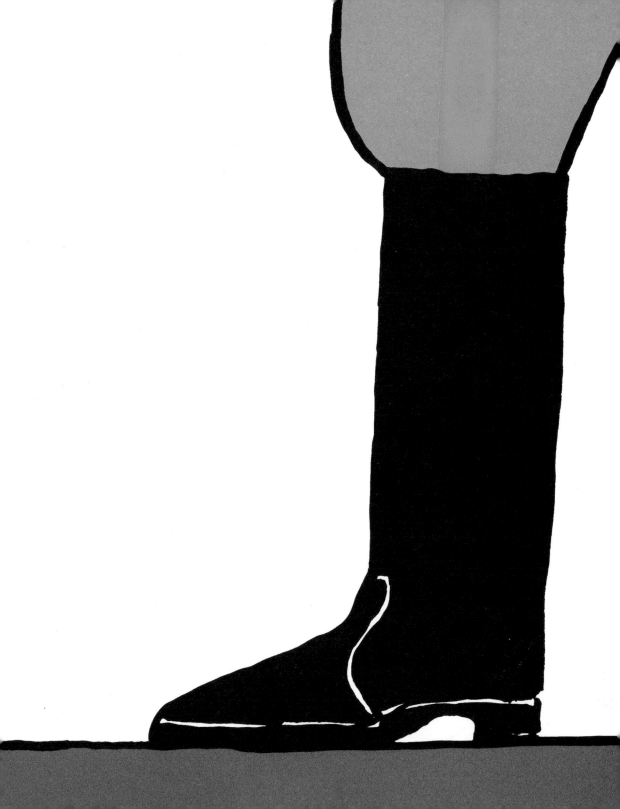

**One,
two,**

where's my shoe?

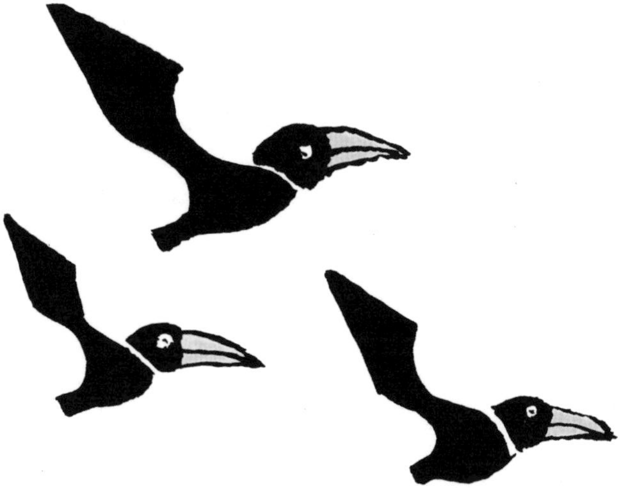

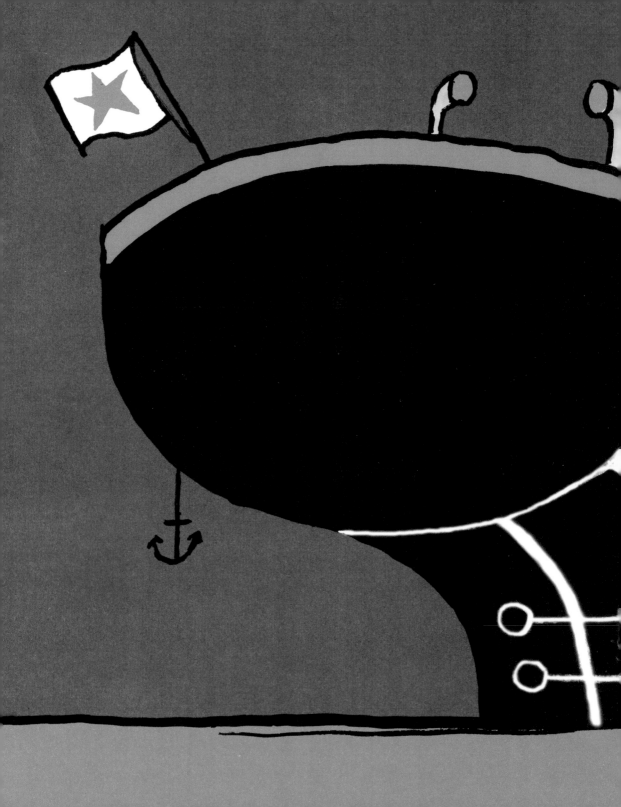

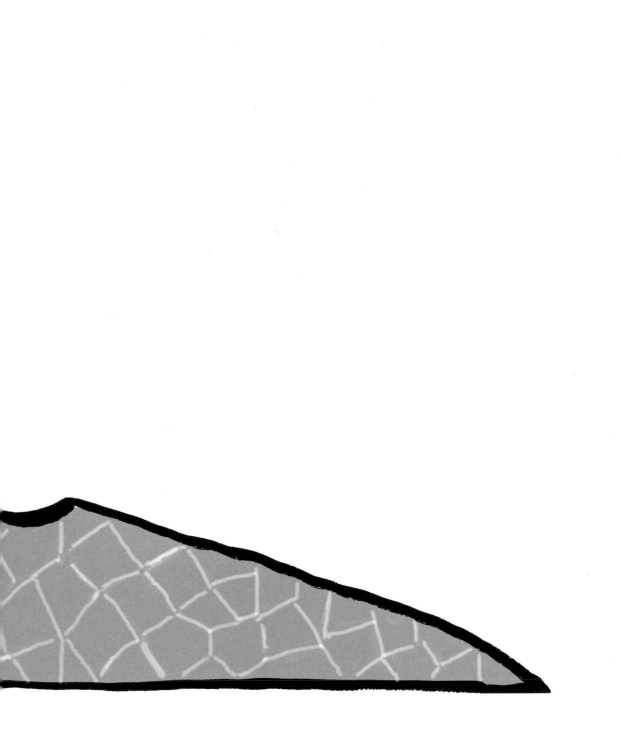

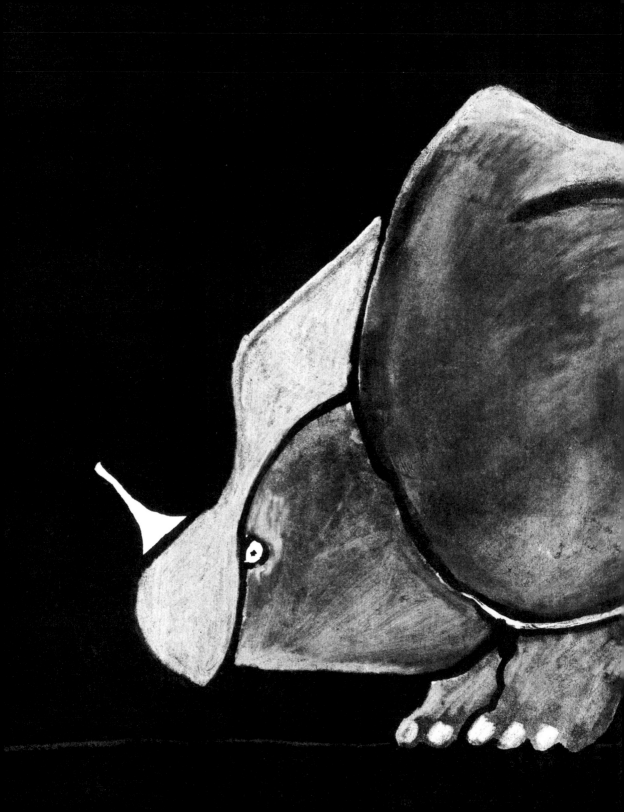

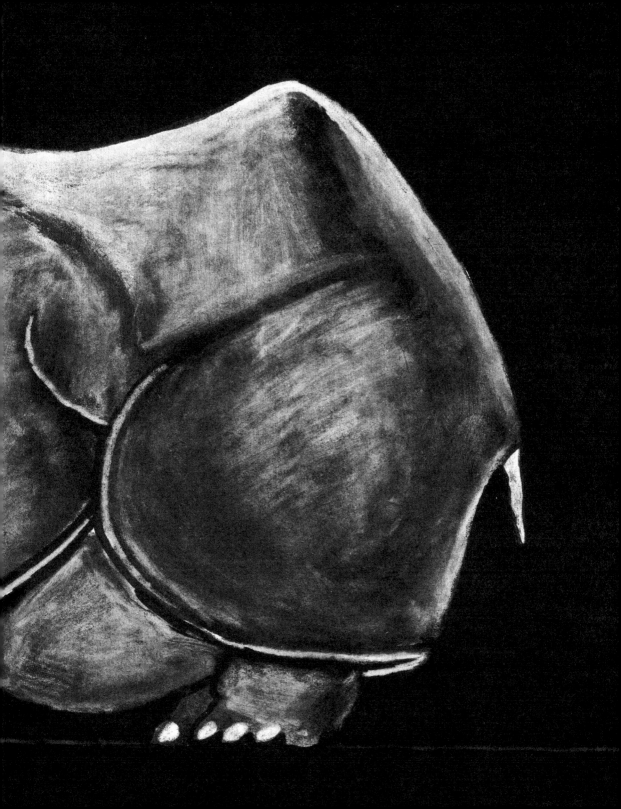

**Three,
four,**

on the floor!

Shoe, where are you? Help find shoe and have fun discovering each hiding place in this witty and wacky game of hide-and-seek.

Tomi Ungerer (b. 1931) is one of the world's most famous and best-loved children's authors. A recipient of the Hans Christian Andersen Award for illustration, he divides his time between Ireland and Strasbourg, France.

Other titles by Tomi Ungerer published by Phaidon:

- Adelaide: The Flying Kangaroo
- The Beast of Monsieur Racine
- Christmas Eve at the Mellops'
- Fog Island
- The Mellops Go Diving for Treasure
- The Mellops Strike Oil
- Moon Man
- No Kiss for Mother
- Otto: The Autobiography of a Teddy Bear
- The Three Robbers

Phaidon Press Limited
Regent's Wharf
All Saints Street
London, N1 9PA

Phaidon Press Inc.
65 Bleecker Street
New York, NY 10012

phaidon.com

This edition © 2014 Phaidon Press Limited
First published in German as Schuh, wo bist du? © 1973 Diogenes Verlag AG Zürich

ISBN 978 0 7148 6798 4
007-0714

A CIP catalogue record for this book is available from the British Library. All rights reserved. No part of this publication may be reproduced, stored in a retrieval system or transmitted, in any form or by any means, electronic, mechanical, photocopying, recording or otherwise, without the written permission of Phaidon Press Limited.

Printed in China